W9-CRZ-928

# Shanyaak'utlaax̲

## Salmon Boy

*Shanyaak'utlaax̱ – Salmon Boy* is an ancient story based on oral history that has been passed from generation to generation for thousands of years. Traditional stories document Native history, reflect Native world-views, and are highly valued clan possessions that are integral to Native identity. This story was adapted from oral accounts into a children's book for Sealaska Heritage's Baby Raven Reads program.

As Richard and Nora Marks Dauenhauer write in the preface to *Haa Shuká, Our Ancestors*, the original stories on which these children's books are based are "not simple children's stories, but adult literature that addresses the 'ambiguities of the human condition' with which we all must come to grips; coming of age as adults, alienation, identity and self concept, conflict of loyalty, pride and arrogance, separation and loss—and many other experiences that are part of being human."

*Shanyaak'utlaax̱ – Salmon Boy* is recognized as a Kiks.ádi story, and versions of this same story are owned by other Raven Clans including the Lukaax̱.ádi. The abbreviated version presented here is a rewrite of the "Salmon Boy Legend" taken from the Juneau Indian Studies Program, 1986. To read the story in its entirety, as told by Deikeenáak'w in 1904, visit: http://www.ankn.uaf.edu/curriculum/Tlingit/Salmon/graphics/swanton.pdf

*"Only in stories and traditions like these do we begin to learn who we are, no matter who we are."*

— *Nora Marks Dauenhauer and Richard Dauenhauer*
preface to *Haa Shuká, Our Ancestors: Tlingit Oral Narratives*

Shanyaak'utlaax – Salmon Boy

This is an update of the 2004 edition published by Sealaska Heritage Institute.
Audio of this text and other language resources may be found online:
http://www.sealaskaheritage.org/institute/education/resources
http://www.sealaskaheritage.org/institute/language/resources

Copyright © 2004, 2017 Sealaska Heritage Institute on behalf of clans that own
the oral tradition and the Northwest Coast tribes who tell this story.
All rights reserved.
Designed in the USA.
Printed in Canada.

Sealaska Heritage Institute
105 S. Seward St. Suite 201
Juneau, Alaska  99801
907.463.4844
www.sealaskaheritage.org

Book design: Nobu Koch

**MIX**
Paper from
responsible sources
**FSC® C016245**
FSC
www.fsc.org

ISBN: 978-1-946019-02-8

10  9  8  7  6  5  4  3  2

This book was made possible through funds from the US Department of Education Alaska Native Education Program Grant
PR# S356A140060 *Raven Reading: A Culturally Responsive Kindergarten Readiness Program*. The contents of this book do not
necessarily represent the policy of the DOE, and you should not assume endorsement by the Federal Government.
Baby Raven Reads is a Sealaska Heritage education program promoting a love of learning through culture and community.

# *Shanyaak'utlaax̱*
## *Salmon Boy*

Johnny Marks, Hans Chester,
David Katzeek, Nora Dauenhauer k̲a
Richard Dauenhauer-ch áwé yax̱ hás ayawsitee

Edited by Johnny Marks, Hans Chester, David Katzeek,
Nora Dauenhauer, and Richard Dauenhauer

Michaela Goade-ch kawshix̱ít

Illustrated by Michaela Goade

SEALASKA
HERITAGE

Ch'áakw áwé haa een has akawlineek
yóo Kiks.ádi atk'átsk'u daat, wé kéidladi
akaawa.áak̲w awooldáas'i.

Long ago, they told us a story about a
Kiks.ádi boy who was trying to snare seagulls.

"Atlée, ax̱ éet yaan uwaháa!" Yéi áwé kei uwa.íx'.

"Atx̱á ax̱ jeet yéi sané!"

Wuditláx̱i x̱áat shanyaa áwé du jéet aawatee wé atk'átsk'u. Kei aawagíx' wé x̱áat shanyaa x'áan tin.

"Ch'a tlákw áwé wuditláx̱i x̱áat ax̱ jeet eetéeych."

"I'm hungry, mom," he yelled to his mother. "Give me something to eat!" She gave him the bony shoulder piece of a dried salmon with mold on the end. The boy flung it away in disgust, saying "You always give me the moldy pieces."

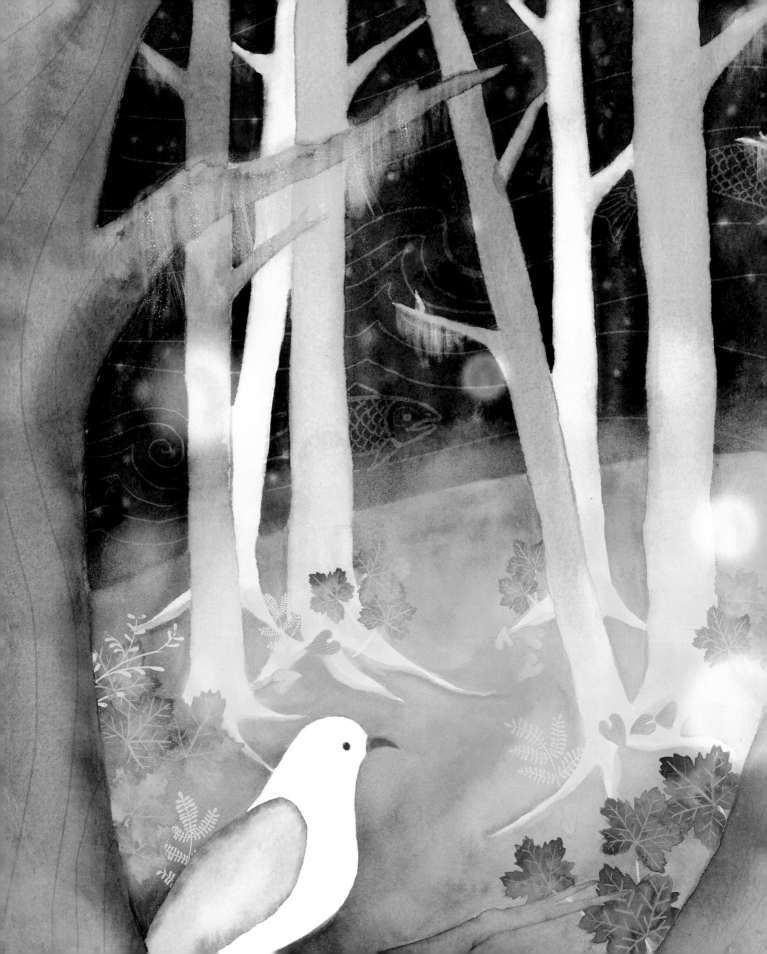

Áx x'ayáa koowdligát.

This is a taboo.

Aagáa áwé kéidladi aawasháat
du dáas'aayi een.

Just then, a seagull was trapped
in his snare. The boy ran down into
the water to pull in the seagull.

Héent kei wjixíx wé atk'átsk'u wé kéidladigaa.
Wé kéidladi ku.aa héen táakde aawaxóot'
wé atk'átsk'u. Deikéet ash uwaxút'.

The seagull kept pulling the snare out into deeper water.

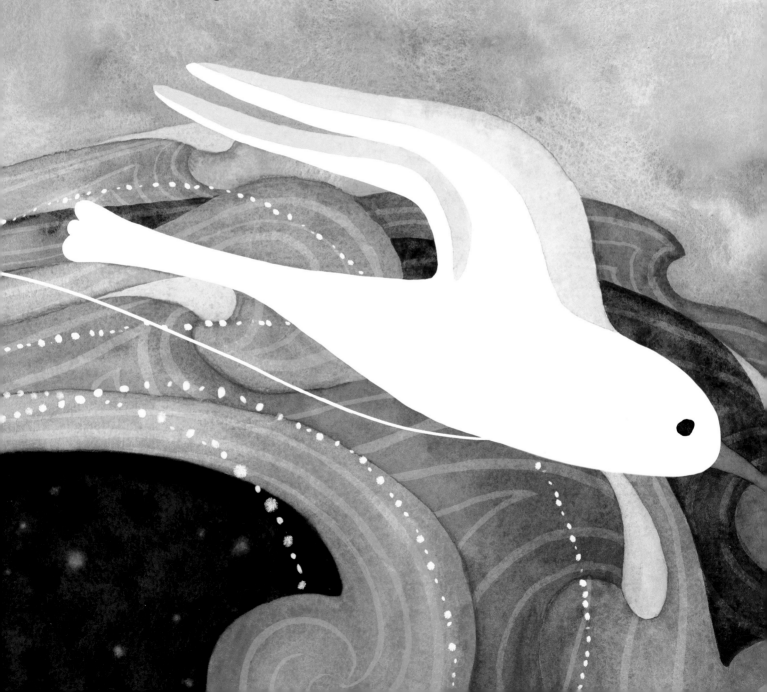

Héen táade wdzigeet wé atk'átsk'u. Áx' áwé
has aawasháat wé X̱áat K̲wáanich k̲u.aa.

The boy was swept under the deep water where
he was brought into the world of the Salmon People.

Aadéi yawakaayí yéich áwé Shanyaak'utlaax yéi
wduwasáa wé Xáat Kwáanich.

They named him Shanyaak'utlaax, or "Moldy End,"
because they were offended by his disrespect.

Daax'oon táakw áwé X̱áat K̲wáani x̲óox' yéi wootee wé atk'átsk'u. Át áwé k̲uwahaa aa has wudix̱eedi yé yéide has yakwgwa.áa.

The boy had been with the Salmon People for four or five years when one day they began moving toward the streams of their birth.

Shanyaak'utlaax̱ du éesh héeni yíkt uwax'ák.

Eventually, Shanyaak'utlaax̱ arrived at his parents' stream.

Du éeshch áwé uwak'éx̱'.

Aadáx̱ du tláa jeet awsitaa.

His father speared him and gave him to his mother.

Du tláach gugaxaashí wé x̱áat,
ayaawatín du yéet seidí.
Ách áyá tlél awuxaash wé x̱áat.

As she was trying to cut the fish,
she saw her son's necklace.
This is why she didn't cut the salmon.

X'oow ḵa x̲'wáal' káa yan has awsitáa.

His father wrapped Shanyaak'utlaax̲ in a blanket.

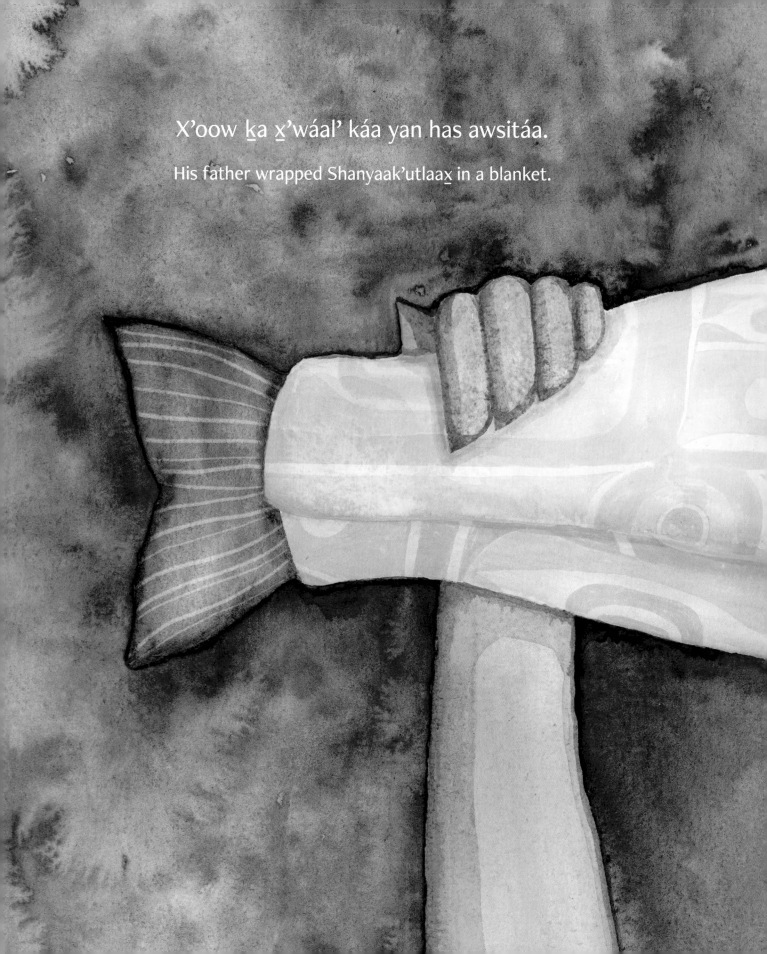

A ítdax̱ áwé Shanyaak'utlaax̱ ḵúx̱ wudigút.
Wé atk'átsk'u du naax̱ satee een akaawanéek
x̱áat daat sh kalneek. Aag̱áa áwé wé x̱áatch
du jeet uwateeyi saa "Aak'wtaatseen."

After a while, Shanyaak'utlaax̱ appeared as a
young man and told his family his story. Then they
named him "Aak'wtaatseen."

Yéi áwé wududzikóo X̱áat Ḵwáanich wusneix̱í.
Atk'átskooch tlél ayáx̱ ayawusḵaa wé x̱áat. Áx̱ x'ayáa
ḵoowulgaadích áwé, X̱áat Ḵwáanich wusineix̱.

He became known as the boy who was captured
by the Salmon People for insulting the Salmon People
and the food that comes from them.

# Artist's Statement

When I first read the text for this Kiks.ádi story, I happened to be in Sitka visiting my parents. I felt a powerful combination of gratitude and magic as I strolled in Totem Park, traditional Kiks.ádi land, and asked for inspiration as I began to create the visual journey of Salmon Boy.

And much like Salmon Boy, I ended up going on a journey of my own and learning a lot about my creative process and style. The opportunity to illustrate a story from my own clan was an amazing first adventure into children's books and I am deeply honored to have been a part of Salmon Boy's story.

Using a mixture of watercolor, gouache, and digital editing techniques, my goal was to create a dream-like and somewhat stylized world that reflects the magic of Tlingit storytelling while staying true to a classic Kiks.ádi tale. My hope is for readers to truly feel and experience the colorful spirit of this story and share in the childlike wonder of Southeast Alaska.

*Michaela Goade* is an illustrator and graphic designer currently residing in Juneau, Alaska. Her Tlingit name is Sheit.een and she is from the Raven moiety and Kiks.ádi Clan from Sitka, Alaska. Raised in Juneau, she spent her childhood in the forests and on the beaches of Southeast Alaska and her artistic style is rooted in the depth and beauty of its landscapes. At the heart of her work, whether it's a logo or book illustration project, is a passion for evocative storytelling. After earning her degrees in graphic design and marketing from Fort Lewis College, she worked as a designer and art director in Anchorage, before embarking on her full-time freelance career and returning to Southeast Alaska.

## about Sealaska Heritage Institute

*Sealaska Heritage Institute* is a regional Native nonprofit 501(c)(3) corporation. Our mission is to perpetuate and enhance Tlingit, Haida, and Tsimshian cultures. Our goal is to promote cultural diversity and cross-cultural understanding.

Sealaska Heritage was founded in 1980 by Sealaska after being conceived by clan leaders, traditional scholars, and Elders at the first Sealaska Elders Conference. During that meeting, the Elders likened Native culture to a blanket. They told the new leaders that their hands were growing weary of holding onto the metaphorical blanket, this "container of wisdom." They said they were transferring this responsibility to Sealaska, the regional Native corporation serving Southeast Alaska. In response, Sealaska founded Sealaska Heritage to operate cultural and educational programs.

## about Baby Raven Reads

Sealaska Heritage sponsors *Baby Raven Reads*, a program that promotes a love of learning through culture and community. The program is for families with Alaska Native children up to age 5. Among other things, events include family nights at the Walter Soboleff Building clan house, Shuká Hít, where families are invited to join us for storytelling, songs, and other cultural activities. Participants also receive free books through the program.

Baby Raven Reads was made possible through funds from the US Department of Education Alaska Native Education Program Grant PR# S356A140060 *Raven Reading: A Culturally Responsive Kindergarten Readiness Program* running from 2015-2017.